By Mary Tillworth
Based on the screenplay by Elise Allen
Illustrated by Ulkutay Design Group

Special thanks to Vicki Jaeger, Monica Okazaki, Ann McNeill, Emily Kelly, Sharon Woloszyk, Julia Phelps,
Tanya Mann, Rob Hudnut, David Wiebe, Shelley Dvi-Vardhana, Michelle Cogan, Rainmaker Entertainment,
Walter P. Martishius, Carla Alford, Rita Lichtwardt, Kathy Berry, and Miranda Nolte

 A GOLDEN BOOK • NEW YORK

Published in the United States by Golden Books, an imprint of Random House Children's Books, a division of Random House,
Inc., 1745 Broadway, New York, NY 10019, and in Canada by Random House of Canada Limited, Toronto. No part of this
book may be reproduced or copied in any form without permission from the copyright owner. Golden Books, A Golden Book,
A Little Golden Book, the G colophon, and the distinctive gold spine are registered trademarks of Random House, Inc.
www.randomhouse.com/kids
Educators and librarians, for a variety of teaching tools, visit us at www.randomhouse.com/teachers
ISBN: 978-0-375-87361-4
Printed in the United States of America
10 9 8 7 6 5 4 3 2 1

It was the first day of class at Princess Charm School in the magical land of Gardania. Young ladies crowded the entrance, eager to begin their lessons. Princess Charm School was a place where royal-born girls learned to become princesses and ordinary girls trained to become Lady Royals, trusted advisors to the princesses.

In a small apartment on the outskirts of Gardania, a lovely waitress named Blair couldn't believe her luck. Her foster sister, Emily, had entered her into the Princess Charm School Contest for the chance to train to be a Lady Royal—and Blair had won!

Blair knew that if she became a Lady Royal, she could provide a better life for her foster mother and sister. So she decided to go.

When Blair arrived at Princess Charm School, she was greeted by Headmistress Privet. The headmistress gave Blair a new uniform and introduced her to a sprite who was flying excitedly through the air. "This is Grace, your sprite."

Blair was overwhelmed. She had never had a personal assistant before!

Blair soon met her two new roommates, Hadley and Isla. "You're hanging out with us," the princesses-in-training said. Blair felt welcome right away, and she was glad to make such good friends.

Blair's first class was taught by Dame Devin, a snobby instructor. Dame Devin explained that years ago, Queen Isabella of Gardania and her family had died in a terrible accident. Dame Devin's daughter, Delancy, was next in line for the throne.

But Isla and Hadley said there were rumors that Isabella's baby, Princess Sophia, had survived!

Dame Devin didn't like Blair competing against her daughter at Princess Charm School. So she told Delancy to do everything she could to make sure that Blair did not succeed. But despite Dame Devin and Delancy's dirty tricks, Blair soon rose to the top of her class.

One day, Dame Devin looked closely at Blair and realized that she was Princess Sophia, who had been missing all these years! To keep her discovery a secret, Dame Devin plotted to get Blair expelled from Princess Charm School.

The next day, Blair and her roommates discovered that their uniforms had been ripped to shreds.

"We're not allowed in class without our uniforms," cried Isla.

"And if we skip a class . . . we will fail Princess Charm School!" Hadley groaned.

Luckily, Blair had an idea. With the help of their personal princess assistants, the girls fashioned new, stylish uniforms out of the torn ones.

The girls raced to class and made it just in time! All their classmates oohed and aahed over their fabulous outfits. Even Headmistress Privet was pleased with the stylish new uniforms. Delancy, however, was jealous and vowed to find a way to get Blair kicked out of Princess Charm School.

A few days later, in Gardania's royal palace, Blair and her friends stumbled upon a portrait of Queen Isabella— *who looked exactly like Blair!*

Blair suddenly realized that she might be Gardania's missing Princess Sophia!

What Blair didn't know was that Delancy had secretly followed her—and now she knew Blair's secret, too!

Shocked by what she had learned, Delancy went to tell
her mother. She found Dame Devin hiding her jewelry
in Blair's room. Dame Devin was going to accuse Blair of
stealing to get her thrown out of Princess Charm School!

Delancy felt torn. She wanted to be Princess of
Gardania, but she knew that Blair was the rightful heir.

When Blair, Hadley, and Isla returned to their room, Dame Devin stormed in. "Arrest them!" she cried.

The stolen jewelry was found underneath the girls' mattresses, and they were sent to the palace dungeon. Dame Devin's wicked plan was working. Blair and her friends would never graduate from Princess Charm School—and Delancy would be crowned Princess of Gardania!

Delancy knew she had to do what was right, so she freed Blair and her friends. She gave the girls a map so they could find the Magical Crown of Gardania. The crown would glow when placed on the head of the true heir to Gardania's throne. Delancy told them to hurry or she would be named Princess of Gardania instead of Blair.

Blair thanked Delancy for all her help.

"I want what's right," said Delancy with a smile.

Using Delancy's map, the girls found the Magical Crown in a huge vault deep within the palace. Suddenly, Dame Devin burst in.

"The crown is *mine*, Blair. You'll never be more than a poor lottery girl." Dame Devin grabbed the crown— and locked the girls in the vault!

Nothing was going to stop the girls from getting Blair
to the coronation ceremony! Isla hummed the tune of the
vault combination. Then the girls typed it into the keypad.
They were free!

Just as Delancy was going to be crowned Princess of Gardania, Blair and her friends burst through the doors. "Wait!" Blair cried.

Dame Devin snarled, "No! Do not wait!"

"I am Princess Sophia, daughter of Queen Isabella!" declared Blair.

Dame Devin grabbed the Magical Crown and tried
to put it on Delancy's head, but Grace and the other
magical sprites tripped her. The crown went flying!
Luckily, the sprites caught the crown and brought
it to Blair.

Everyone held their breath as the crown was placed on Blair's head. The crown began to glow brighter and brighter, and Blair's dress was magically transformed into a beautiful royal gown. Blair really *was* Princess Sophia, the true ruler of Gardania!

"You useless child!" Dame Devin screamed at Delancy. "I eliminated Queen Isabella so you could be princess!"

Dame Devin was so furious, she didn't realize that she had just confessed her evil plot in front of the television cameras. In moments, news of Dame Devin's treachery and the return of Gardania's lost princess was everywhere!

Then Blair spoke for the first time as Princess Sophia. "I'm just a regular girl. But I think Headmistress Privet is right when she says every girl has princess potential. I promise to always work hard, and to be just and kind."

Blair then turned to Delancy and asked her to be her Lady Royal. "I wouldn't be wearing this crown without your help. Will you accept?"

"I would be honored, Your Highness," said Delancy happily.

Just then, Blair's foster mom and sister arrived. Emily was overjoyed to be at the palace. "If you're a princess . . . does that mean I'm a princess, too?" she asked Blair.

"You've always been a princess," Blair said with a laugh. And she led her family into their new royal home.